To Amber
I hope you enjoy my book !!
from Ian x

The Mystery Present

by Ian Beresford

Grosvenor House
Publishing Limited

This book is published by
Grosvenor House Publishing Ltd
Link House
140 The Broadway, Tolworth, Surrey, KT6 7HT.
www.grosvenorhousepublishing.co.uk

A CIP record for this book
is available from the British Library

ISBN 978-1-83975-434-0

Dedication

I dedicate this story to my friends, family and especially to my wife Melly, who had to put up with listening to countless ideas on a similar theme and having to read numerous drafts over a long period of time.

In a house on the edge of open woodland, and not far from the nearest town, there lived Mr and Mrs Pemberton and their eleven-year-old son, Oliver.

As a family, they took pleasure in all that the surrounding countryside could offer. Sometimes, if Oliver was not at home, Mr and Mrs Pemberton were content just to sit and enjoy the splendour of their garden. This activity particularly appealed to Mr Pemberton, as, unlike so many things, it cost nothing.

Oliver was a caring young boy. At every opportunity, he would lend a helping hand to anyone who needed it. Typically, there were some who were ready to take advantage of his kindness.

"I should use that boy to do my household chores," remarked the local busybody to her long-suffering neighbour. "That way, I could spend more time poking my nose into other people's business."

"I don't care for your attitude!" responded the neighbour. "If you earn someone's kindness or trust through deception or self-interest, sooner or later the truth will be revealed, and you'll have to face the consequences."

"You are right," murmured the busybody unconvincingly, and she scuttled away, clearly intent on stirring up more bad feeling elsewhere.

For Oliver, no job was more satisfying than caring for his father's fine collection of antique clocks. Many in the collection had passed down through the Pemberton family over several generations. Others, his father had bought from Mr Schiller, a clock dealer, whose shop was located amid medieval buildings and cobblestoned alleys in the nearby town centre.

Mr Schiller had been selling and repairing antique clocks for as long as he could remember. Old-fashioned in his appearance, he possessed a charm and elegance that matched so well the nature of his business. Recognising that many of today's collectibles will become tomorrow's antiques, he also sold a range of modern quality clocks and mechanical wristwatches; repairs to these, were normally carried out by the makers themselves.

Caring for the Pemberton clocks occupied much of Oliver's free time. Every morning before school, Oliver would dash from room to room winding up the timepieces and adjusting their hands if one or other was running fast or slow. If any needed repair, he, or his father, would pay a visit to Mr Schiller's shop. At weekends, Oliver would often dust or even polish the various pieces. It was then that he would marvel at the complex engineering and the sheer beauty of many in the collection.

One day, Mr Pemberton returned home early from work in an unusually good mood. That is not to say he was always in a bad mood, but that sometimes he could be rather grumpy, depending on how his day had gone.

"Oliver," he said, handing him a small wrapped object, "this is a present for you. It is something your mother and I know you will appreciate now and for many years to come. Think of it as a reward for looking after my clocks with so much dedication and enthusiasm."

Full of excitement, Oliver sat at the kitchen table and immediately started to tear open the present or 'mystery present', as he preferred to call it.

In an instant, he was gazing in awe at the most magnificent watch he had ever seen. It was elegant, highly fashionable and very sporty. From the packaging, Oliver knew at once it had been bought from Mr Schiller.

"Wow! This watch is amazing!" cried Oliver, as he reached out to hug his parents. "Thank you, thank you a million times!"

"It's certainly no ordinary watch," Mr Pemberton declared. "Only a relatively small number were made. Watches that are limited in number are highly desirable, especially to collectors. Mr Schiller and the many other dealers would have been allocated just a few of these watches each. I happened to be in the shop at the right time. And my good fortune did not end there. Because the watchmaker regards these watches to be his best creation yet, he told Mr Schiller that if they developed a fault of any kind, whatever their age, he would personally repair them free of charge.

Yes Oliver, free of charge! I could hardly believe my ears! Of course, since you are now the rightful owner, this benefit will pass to you."

"I can't believe my ears or my eyes!" Oliver replied, winding the movement and adjusting the hands to the correct time. "I'll treasure this watch for ever!"

By the time Oliver was twelve, he had become quite an authority on the study of clocks and watches, or horology as it is sometimes called. Much of his knowledge he owed to Mr Schiller, who would regularly invite him to his shop during the school holidays.

It was on one of these occasions, that Oliver received word that his father had collapsed in the garden and had been taken to hospital. The incident came as a great shock to Oliver; his father was young and had no history of ill-health. In a moment of reflection, a strange feeling crept over him and he sensed at once that he needed to return home as fast as he could. On reaching the house, he noticed his mother standing at the front door, supported by two friends. Straightaway, she rushed to embrace him. Overcome by grief, she could barely speak. "Oliver, there's no easy way to break this to you, but I'm afraid your father suffered a turn for the worse and sadly died a short time ago. It was all very sudden and unexpected." As she spoke, Oliver's eyes filled with tears and he clung to his mother's arms as if he would never let go. Repeatedly he sought an explanation, but each time his probing questions fell on deaf ears. Eventually, the two friends discreetly slipped away, and Oliver and his mother entered the house closing the door gently behind them.

In the weeks that followed, Oliver and his mother held on to their memories by staying at home and seeing no one. However, as time passed, both came to adapt to their new circumstances and move forward with their lives. Throughout, Oliver managed to continue his routine of caring for the timepieces, while his mother pottered about in the garden more than ever.

One morning, when Oliver was carrying out his usual horological checks, he noticed that the watch his father had given him had stopped working. Tapping and shaking it seemed to make no difference and he soon realised that he would have to call on the watchmaker to have it repaired.

Oliver saw no point in delaying things unnecessarily. Indeed, the very next day, he set off on foot to visit the watchmaker's workshop. This was located at a business centre forty minutes from home, or at least, that is what he thought; whatever his reasoning, he needed no reminding that the watch he was wearing was currently incapable of indicating his true journey time.

The watchmaker's premises were spread over a large area and finding the right place to go proved challenging. Quite by chance, Oliver discovered that the watchmaker was based not in a workshop at all, but in a huge barn complex converted into offices. Once inside, he was directed up numerous flights of stairs and along endless corridors until finally he came to a door on which was written, 'Mr Swindledorf: Watchmaker Extraordinaire.' After being allowed to enter, Oliver faced a stout and elderly gentleman seated at a desk. Every free space was littered with papers and on a small table sat an ashtray heaped in cigar butts. Most notably, and to Oliver's astonishment, there was not a watch to be seen anywhere.

"What can I do for you?" Mr Swindledorf asked in a gruff voice and peering over his half-moon spectacles. "Be quick, I'm very busy!"

Rather taken aback by the watchmaker's abruptness, Oliver began timidly to explain the reason for his visit. "I've come here today," he announced, "because my watch is not working and needs repairing under the terms specified at the time of purchase."

"And what might those terms be?" Mr Swindledorf demanded.

"Why, for you to repair the watch free of charge," replied Oliver.

"Free of charge!" the watchmaker cried, almost falling off his chair in horror. "That could never be. I would be out of business in no time. Anyway, it wouldn't be me who repairs your watch; I have people to do that for me."

"But free repairs are what my father understood when he bought the watch," Oliver insisted. "You cannot go back on your word!"

"Then it's the dealer who's at fault, not me!" snapped Mr Swindledorf angrily. " Besides, even if I did say the things you say I said, and I know I didn't, there is nothing in writing to say that I did, so, as far as I'm concerned, that's the end of it."

From the watchmaker's tone of voice, Oliver foresaw that things could become very awkward for Mr Schiller if he pursued the matter any longer. As things stood, Mr Swindledorf had no idea where the watch was bought, and it seemed to Oliver that it was best to keep it that way. He therefore hastily gathered his belongings and left without so much as a goodbye.

Oliver was naturally saddened by the outcome. After all, he was still in possession of a watch that needed repair. If he had gained anything, it was the realisation that he had no desire to see the disagreeable watchmaker ever again. It was also obvious to Oliver that what Mr Swindledorf had told Mr Schiller was nothing more than a ploy to promote the sale of his watches.

On the long walk back, the disheartened Oliver came to rest on the steps of an old courthouse in the town square. It was there that he hoped for inspiration on what to do next. Unfortunately, the more he thought, the more he thought his head was emptying of any thoughts at all.

Then, just before he was about to give up and go home, Oliver caught a glimpse of the town's mayor walking in his direction. The mayor was known to be extremely wise, and it occurred to Oliver that such an influential person might be able to offer him some useful advice.

"Excuse me Mr Mayor," Oliver murmured nervously, "I've been wronged on a matter that has affected me greatly, and I wonder could you please advise me on what I should do."

"You are the Pemberton boy if I am not mistaken," the mayor replied, stooping down to shake Oliver's hand. "I knew your father very well. Walk with me and tell me what troubles you."

Oliver, grateful for the mayor's attention, immediately began to describe in detail his ordeal with Mr Swindledorf. When he had finished, he waited eagerly to hear what the mayor had to say.

"Your story is all too familiar," the mayor confessed. "Unfortunately, there are people in this world who say one thing and do another. If, as you say, there is nothing in writing to back your case, then I fear you must put this whole episode behind you. However, you can take comfort in the fact that you have acted honourably. Not only to your father, by standing your ground on what you believe to be right, but also to Mr Schiller, by protecting his business interests with the watchmaker. These are infinitely greater

accomplishments than securing free repairs of your watch. Be assured, your watch can and will be mended, but you must be patient. I now have to leave you; I've urgent business to attend to."

After Oliver had thanked the mayor for his much-needed advice and encouragement, Oliver began his walk home. On the way, he gave much consideration to what the mayor had said. It seemed to Oliver that the priority now was to find someone else willing to repair the watch. Suddenly, the thought came to him that his friend, Mr Schiller, might hold the solution. Oliver wasted no time. He turned on his heels and headed back to town.

Mr Schiller was so excited to see Oliver enter the shop.

"Oliver, I've just had the pleasure of a visit from the mayor. He has told me all about your unfortunate dealings with Mr Swindledorf. The mayor has given you good advice. I too have something to tell you.

What you have experienced today is typical of the challenges we all face every day of our lives. Your challenge was a test of your loyalty to your father and to me. Whether it was by chance that you saw the mayor today, or coincidence that you are here now, who can say. But such uncertainties make me think that you would do well to try to understand what led you to act in the manner that you did. Learn from this lesson. Always stay true to your word, and never deceive or take advantage of others. This way, your aims and desires are more likely to be fulfilled."

As Oliver was mulling over all that had been said, Mr Schiller suddenly gestured to Oliver to tell him the time. Oliver, glancing at his watch, waited a moment, then announced "it's twenty past five exactly."

"Just as I thought," said Mr Schiller, "your watch is running perfectly."

For a second or two, Oliver stood transfixed, mystified at what had happened. Then, having reassured himself that his watch was indeed ticking away happily, he leapt into the air with joy. "What magic!" he shouted, looking at Mr Schiller in disbelief. "My watch is working again!"

"I doubt it is magic that has restored your watch," replied Mr Schiller; "I would suggest there is a deeper or,

perhaps, even a simpler explanation. However, you must unlock the mystery for yourself."

And with that, Mr Schiller bade Oliver a fond farewell until another day and closed the shop.

The next morning, Oliver awoke later than normal. At first, he looked lost in thought, but then, in a flash, he threw off the bedclothes and ran with haste to check his watch. Immediately, a broad smile came across his face, for he had discovered the truth about the events that had occurred the previous day.

THE END

About the Author - Ian Beresford

On completion of a post-graduate qualification in music at London University, Ian Beresford spent the next fourteen years first working in shipping and later in the horseracing industry. Alongside his work, he continued his passion for singing and joined the Philharmonia Chorus of London in 1977. In the roughly 25 years with the Chorus, he took part in many historic performances, not only in the UK, but also in Europe and the United States. These included London Hyde Park in 1991, with Luciano Pavarotti, La Scala Milan in 1990, with Carlo Maria Giulini, and the Vatican in 2000, in the presence of Pope John Paul II on his 80th birthday.

In 1993, Ian began to devote most of his time to piano teaching. Having largely an international clientele based in the UK, his teaching has recently developed into virtual lessons stretching as far as Australia. Outside of work, Ian's other interests include classic cars, travel and vintage wristwatches from the Art Deco period.

About the Illustrator - Julie Sneeden

Constantly inspired by the words and tales of imaginative authors, Julie Sneeden uses colour, light and creativity to bring her illustrations, sketches and paintings into these magical worlds. To make the character of her images come to life, she is able to draw upon a palette of different tools including watercolour, pencil, charcoal, digital illustration, photography and oil paints.

Julie Sneeden studied Fine Arts in KwaZulu Natal, South Africa, but now lives in the UK with her husband and four children. Although she does work as a Graphic Designer and Artist, reading stories to her children has inspired her over the years to pursue the Art of Book Illustration. She has illustrated numerous stories to amazing authors all over the world.

CPSIA information can be obtained
at www.ICGtesting.com
Printed in the USA
LVHW071545120421
684234LV00012B/130